Nuts About You

Hillary A. Hinds

Nuts About You

Copyright© 2020 by Hillary A. Hinds

All Scripture quotations are taken from the Holy Bible, King James Version, which is in the public domain.
ISBN: 978-1-7771012-2-0
Written by Hillary A. Hinds, Books4dNations Learning Innovations.
Cover and book illustrations by StallionStudios88
Publisher by Hillary A. Hinds, Books4dNations Learning Innovations
Cataloguing in Publication may be obtained through Library and Archives Canada.

To the Nations' Kids

Love

Hillary

Nuts About You is a funny story about love and courage that will inspire young readers as they read.

I am nuts about you
everywhere I go.

I am nuts about you all
the time.

I am nuts about you
when I am scared.
I am nuts about you
when I am brave.

I am nuts about you,
wintertime and
summertime.

I am nuts about you, all
season long.

I am nuts about you when I am going round and round.

I am nuts about you when I am falling.

I am nuts about you
because you are funny.

I am nuts about you
because you care.

I am nuts about you when
I am blue.

I am nuts about you when
I am glad.

I am nuts about you every day.

I am nuts about you even when you are there.

I am nuts about you
when it rains.

I am nuts about you
when it's sunny.

I am nuts about you when

I am in the clouds.

I am nuts about you

seeing clearly.

I am nuts about you when
I am going up and down.

I am nuts about you when
I am going through the
town.

I am nuts about you
when I am going around
the world.

I am nuts about you when
I am going to the moon.

I am nuts about you when
I am on the ground.
I am nuts about you when
I am in a tree.

I am nuts about you
when I am weak.

I am nuts about you
when I am strong.

I am nuts about you;

can't you see.

I am nuts about you!

Let all your things be done in charity.

1 Corinthians 16:14

KJV.

About the Author

Hillary A. Hinds is the author of the children's books *Rabbit Goes to Church*, *Blessings from Above*, *Mama Bear Knows Best* and *It's My Time* inspirational journal. She was born in Jamaica and currently resides in Canada.

Hillary is the founder of Books4NAtionsKids of Saskatchewan, which provides faith-based books to kids and to different charities worldwide.